DIAMOND
HEIST

On 47th Street, New York City

Dr. Maxwell Shimba

Printed by Shimba Publishing LLC
Printed in the United States of America

TABLE OF CONTENTS

PREFACE

In the heart of New York City lies a bustling enclave known as the Diamond District, where the glitter of gemstones and the hum of business converge in a vibrant symphony. This single block on 47th Street is a world unto itself, a place where fortunes are made and lost, and where every transaction holds a story. It is here, amidst the brilliance of diamonds and the shadows they cast, that our story unfolds.

The New York Diamond Heist on 47th Street is a tale of intrigue, ambition, and the relentless pursuit of justice. It is a story that delves deep into the complex web of crime and corruption, unraveling the lives of those who inhabit this unique corner of the city. At its core, this is a story about people—those who uphold the law, those who break it, and those who walk the fine line in between.

Our protagonists, Detective James Walker and Detective Sarah Martinez, are two of New York's finest. They are seasoned detectives, each bringing their own strengths, experiences, and motivations to the table. Walker, with his sharp intuition and unwavering determination, and Martinez, with her analytical mind and compassionate heart, form a formidable partnership. Together, they navigate the challenges and dangers of their profession, driven by a shared commitment to justice.

The antagonist, Marcus Kane, is a criminal mastermind whose brilliance is matched only by his elusiveness. Kane represents the darker side of ambition—a man who uses his intelligence and resources to orchestrate one of the most audacious heists in the history of the Diamond District. His meticulous planning and cunning make him a formidable foe, one who pushes our detectives to their limits.

Throughout this narrative, we witness the unfolding of a grand scheme through the eyes of those who seek to thwart it. The small-scale thefts and suspicious activities that mark the beginning of the heist set the stage for a high-stakes game of cat and mouse. As the plot thickens, alliances are tested, secrets are revealed, and the true extent of the criminal network comes to light.

The story also explores the broader implications of crime and justice, highlighting the interplay between power, greed, and morality. It delves into the sacrifices made by those who choose to stand against corruption, and the personal toll that such a commitment entails. Through the lens of Walker and Martinez, we see the human side of law enforcement—the dedication, the struggles, and the unyielding hope for a better future.

This book is not just a chronicle of a heist; it is a reflection on the nature of good and evil, and the gray areas that exist in between. It is an exploration of the lengths to which people will go to achieve their desires and the resilience of those who strive to uphold the law in the face of overwhelming odds.

As you turn the pages, you will be drawn into a world where every detail matters, every character has a story, and every decision carries weight. The New York Diamond Heist on 47th Street is a journey into the heart of a city that never sleeps, where the line between right and wrong is constantly blurred, and where the pursuit of justice is both a duty and a calling.

Welcome to the Diamond District. Welcome to the story of a heist that shook New York City and the detectives who brought it to light.

DR. MAXWELL SHIMBA

CHAPTER 01

THE SETUP

The Diamond District on 47th Street in Manhattan was always alive with a certain kind of sparkle that went beyond the glittering gems showcased in every window. The air buzzed with the hum of busy traders, the chatter of international clients, and the constant clink of gold and diamonds being weighed and appraised. It was a place where fortunes were made and lost, and where every transaction carried the weight of a thousand whispered secrets.

Detective James Walker navigated the crowded street with the ease of someone who had spent years walking these same few blocks. Tall and broad-shouldered, with a face that bore the lines of countless sleepless nights and a gaze that missed nothing, he was a seasoned veteran of the NYPD. His presence alone commanded respect, but it was his sharp intellect and relentless pursuit of justice that truly set him apart.

Beside him walked Detective Sarah Martinez, her dark hair pulled back into a practical ponytail, her eyes scanning the crowd with a mix of curiosity and caution. Sarah was newer to the force, but her tenacity and keen observational skills had quickly earned her a reputation. She had a knack for seeing connections that others missed, and her partnership with Walker had proven to be a formidable one.

Today, the pair were in the Diamond District following up on a series of small-scale thefts that had been reported over the past few weeks. Individually, the incidents seemed insignificant – a missing ring here, a misplaced necklace there – but Walker's gut told him there was more to the story.

"Another report came in this morning," Sarah said, flipping through her notes as they walked. "A jeweler on 48th reported a missing shipment of loose diamonds. No sign of forced entry."

Walker nodded, his mind already racing through the possibilities. "Sounds like our thief is getting bolder. Or more desperate."

Sarah glanced up at him. "You think it's connected to the other thefts?"

"Too many coincidences in too short a time frame," Walker replied. "Someone's testing the waters, seeing how far they can push before we catch on."

As they continued down the street, Walker's eyes fell on a figure standing in the shadows of a narrow alleyway. The man was tall and lean, dressed in a dark coat that blended into the dim light. His eyes followed the detectives with a keen, almost predatory interest.

Marcus Kane watched Walker and Martinez with a slight smile playing on his lips. A mastermind in the world of high-stakes crime, Marcus was known for his meticulous planning and uncanny ability to stay one step ahead of the law. He had been operating in the shadows of the Diamond District for months, carefully laying the groundwork for his most ambitious heist yet.

Marcus had grown up in the rough neighborhoods of New York, where survival depended on cunning and ruthlessness. Over the years, he had honed his skills, becoming a ghost in the criminal underworld. His operations were flawless, his heists legendary, and his identity a mystery to all but a select few.

As he watched the detectives, Marcus's mind raced with possibilities. He knew they were good – Walker, especially, had a reputation for being a bloodhound when it came to sniffing out crime. But Marcus was confident in his plan. Every detail had been accounted for, every contingency prepared.

The recent thefts were just the beginning, small tests to gauge the district's response and identify any weaknesses in security. The real prize lay ahead – a vault containing millions of dollars' worth of uncut diamonds. Marcus had spent months studying the vault's security system, learning the routines of the guards, and acquiring the specialized equipment needed to breach its defenses.

For now, he remained patient, waiting for the perfect moment to strike. He turned away from the alley and melted back into the crowd, confident that his presence had gone unnoticed.

As Walker and Martinez reached the end of the street, Sarah sighed. "I feel like we're missing something. These thefts don't add up."

"They will," Walker said, his voice firm. "We just need to keep digging. Someone's getting ready for something big, and when they make their move, we'll be ready."

The detectives continued their patrol, unaware that they were already being watched by the very criminal they sought. The Diamond District, with all its glittering wealth and hidden dangers, was about to become the stage for a heist that would test their skills and their resolve like never before. And in the shadows, Marcus Kane smiled, knowing that the game was just beginning.

CHAPTER 02

THE HESIST PLAN

In a dimly lit warehouse on the outskirts of Brooklyn, Marcus Kane stood before a large table covered with blueprints, photographs, and schematics. The walls were lined with high-tech equipment, and the air buzzed with tense anticipation. His team, a carefully selected group of specialists, gathered around him, each one playing a crucial role in the heist to come.

Marcus looked at each member of his crew, his eyes reflecting a cold determination. There was Ryan, the tech genius who could hack into any security system with a few keystrokes. Beside him stood Carla, a master of disguise and infiltration. Across the table, Sam, an expert safecracker with nerves of steel, studied the blueprints intently. Finally, there was Big Joe, the muscle of the group, whose imposing presence was enough to deter any potential threats.

"Alright, everyone," Marcus began, his voice calm but commanding. "We've been planning this for months, and now it's time to put everything into action. We know the vault's layout, the guards' schedules, and the security protocols. This is our one shot, and we can't afford any mistakes."

Ryan tapped on his laptop, bringing up a detailed map of the Diamond District. "I've managed to access the building's security feed. We'll have a thirty-minute window when the guards change shifts. That's our best chance to get in and out without being detected."

Carla nodded, her eyes narrowing as she reviewed the photographs of the guards. "I've got their uniforms and IDs ready. We'll blend in, and no one will suspect a thing."

Sam leaned over the table, tracing the route they would take. "The vault is protected by a state-of-the-art locking system. I've got the tools to bypass it, but it'll take time. We'll need to keep the area clear while I work."

Big Joe cracked his knuckles, a grin spreading across his face. "Leave that to me. Anyone gets in our way, they won't know what hit them."

Marcus smiled, satisfied with their readiness. He pulled out a detailed sketch of the vault, highlighting the critical points. "Remember, the diamonds are stored in the inner vault. Once we're inside, we'll need to move quickly. Ryan, you'll handle the security systems. Carla, you and Joe will secure the perimeter. Sam, you're with me on the vault."

The team nodded, their confidence bolstered by Marcus's leadership. They had worked together on smaller jobs before, but this was their biggest score yet. The risk was high, but so was the reward.

As they finalized their plans, Marcus's mind drifted back to the detectives he had seen earlier. He knew they would be a problem, but he also relished the challenge. Outsmarting the NYPD's finest would make the victory even sweeter.

"All right, everyone," Marcus said, snapping back to the present. "Get some rest. Tomorrow night, we make history."

The team dispersed, each member preparing for their role in the heist. Marcus stayed behind, his eyes fixed on the blueprints. He knew every detail, every possible obstacle. Yet, there was always the unpredictability of human error and unforeseen circumstances. He couldn't shake the feeling that something might go wrong.

Meanwhile, back at the precinct, Walker and Sarah were piecing together the clues from the recent thefts. They had mapped out the locations and timelines, but the pattern remained elusive.

"There's a method to this madness," Walker muttered, studying the board filled with photographs and notes. "These aren't random thefts. Someone's planning something big."

Sarah leaned against the desk, deep in thought. "We need to find the connection. What's the common thread?"

Just then, Rachel walked into the precinct, her face pale and anxious. She held a small package in her hands, which she placed on Walker's desk.

"I think this might help," she said, her voice trembling slightly. "I found this outside my shop this morning."

Walker opened the package, revealing a small device and a note. The device was a high-tech jammer, capable of disrupting security systems. The note contained a single word: "Tomorrow."

Walker's eyes widened. "This is it. They're making their move tomorrow night."

Sarah grabbed her coat. "We need to warn the district and prepare for the heist. If we can catch them in the act, we'll finally put an end to this."

Walker nodded, adrenaline pumping through his veins. "Let's get to work."

As the sun set over New York City, the Diamond District remained oblivious to the impending danger. The streets, bustling with activity, slowly began to quiet as night fell. The stage was set, the players were in position, and the clock was ticking.

Marcus stood by the window of the warehouse, gazing out at the city skyline. He felt a thrill of anticipation mixed with a sliver of anxiety. This heist would either cement his reputation as a criminal mastermind or be his undoing.

Taking a deep breath, he turned to his team. "It's time. Let's do this."

The team moved with precision, their actions synchronized like a well-oiled machine. They navigated the dark streets, slipping into the shadows, ready to execute their plan. The Diamond District, with all its wealth and allure, was about to be rocked by a heist unlike any other.

And in the heart of it all, Detective James Walker and Detective Sarah Martinez prepared for the battle ahead, determined to protect their city and bring the criminals to justice.

CHAPTER 03

UNLIKELY ALLIES

The sun rose over Manhattan, casting a golden glow on the Diamond District. Jewelers opened their shops, security guards began their shifts, and the street slowly came to life with the usual hustle and bustle. But beneath the surface, tensions simmered. The police had quietly increased their presence, ready for the heist they knew was coming.

Detective James Walker stood at the precinct's window, sipping his coffee as he surveyed the district below. His partner, Detective Sarah Martinez, was poring over the surveillance footage from the past week, searching for any clue that might give them an edge.

"We need more eyes on the ground," Walker said, turning to Sarah. "Whatever Marcus Kane is planning, it's going to be big. We can't afford to miss anything."

Sarah nodded, her eyes tired but determined. "I've contacted all our informants in the area. If anyone sees something, we'll know."

Just then, the door to the office opened, and Rachel walked in, her face pale with worry. She was a jeweler who had become an unexpected ally in their investigation. Her knowledge of the Diamond District was invaluable, and her courage to step forward had already provided critical information.

"Detective Walker, Detective Martinez," she greeted them, her voice slightly shaky. "I need to talk to you."

Walker motioned for her to sit. "What is it, Rachel?"

She took a deep breath, trying to steady herself. "Last night, after I left here, I found another note outside my shop. It was from Marcus Kane. He wants to meet."

Sarah's eyebrows shot up. "Meet? Why would he want to meet with you?"

Rachel handed over the note. "He said he has a proposition for me. Something about helping him with the heist."

Walker read the note, his mind racing. This was unexpected. "He must think you can provide him with something he needs. But why would he risk exposure by contacting you directly?"

Rachel looked down, her hands trembling. "I don't know. But I think he's getting desperate. Maybe something in his plan isn't going as smoothly as he thought."

Walker exchanged a glance with Sarah. This could be the break they needed. "Rachel, do you think you can handle this? It's dangerous, but if you're willing, this could be our best chance to catch him."

Rachel looked up, her eyes filled with determination. "I'll do it. I want to help bring him down."

Later that evening, Rachel stood nervously in a small café on the edge of the Diamond District. The place was nearly empty, the low hum of conversation and the clinking of dishes the only sounds. She had arrived early, her eyes scanning every face that walked in.

Marcus Kane entered the café with the ease of someone who owned the place. He spotted Rachel and made his way to her table, his expression calm and confident.

"Rachel," he greeted her, sitting down without waiting for an invitation. "Thank you for meeting me."

Rachel forced a smile. "You left me little choice."

Marcus chuckled, leaning back in his chair. "True. But I believe this meeting will be beneficial for both of us."

Rachel steeled herself, trying to project confidence. "What do you want from me, Marcus?"

He leaned forward, his eyes narrowing. "I need access to a specific jeweler's vault. It's heavily secured, and your connections could help me get inside."

Rachel's mind raced. She had to play this carefully. "And why would I help you?"

Marcus's smile faded, replaced by a cold, calculating look. "Because if you don't, your shop and everyone you care about could become collateral damage in what's about to happen. But if you cooperate, you'll be generously rewarded."

Rachel felt a chill run down her spine. "All right. What do you need me to do?"

Marcus handed her a small device. "This is a jammer. It will disable the security system for exactly fifteen minutes.

Place it near the vault entrance at midnight, and my team will take care of the rest."

Rachel nodded, taking the device with trembling hands. "Okay. I'll do it."

Marcus's smile returned, warmer this time. "Good. Remember, Rachel, I'm counting on you."

Back at the precinct, Rachel recounted the entire conversation to Walker and Sarah. The detectives listened intently, their expressions growing grimmer by the second.

Walker leaned back in his chair, deep in thought. "This changes everything. If we can use this jammer to our advantage, we might be able to catch Marcus and his team in the act."

Sarah nodded. "But we need to be careful. If Marcus suspects anything, he'll bolt, and we'll lose our chance."

Walker turned to Rachel, his expression serious. "You did great, Rachel. Now we need you to do one more thing. Plant the jammer as instructed, but make sure you're out of there before midnight. We'll handle the rest."

Rachel nodded, feeling a mix of fear and resolve. "I understand. I'll do it."

As Rachel left the precinct, Walker and Sarah began to lay out their plan. They coordinated with their team, ensuring every detail was covered. The trap was set, and all they could do now was wait.

The night of the heist, the Diamond District was eerily quiet. Security guards patrolled their usual routes, unaware of the storm about to descend. Hidden in the shadows, the NYPD team waited, their nerves on edge.

Rachel placed the jammer as instructed, her heart pounding. She slipped away into the night, praying that everything would go as planned.

At exactly midnight, the jammer activated, plunging the security systems into chaos. Marcus and his team moved swiftly, entering the building with practiced precision.

Walker and Sarah watched from their hidden vantage point, ready to move at a moment's notice. The next few minutes would determine the success of their entire operation.

As Marcus and his team approached the vault, Sam began to work on the lock, his fingers moving with incredible speed and dexterity. Just as the vault door began to open, Walker gave the signal.

"Now!"

The NYPD team sprang into action, surrounding Marcus and his crew. A tense standoff ensued, weapons drawn and nerves taut.

Marcus's eyes flickered with surprise and anger. "Walker. I should have known."

Walker stepped forward, his gun trained on Marcus. "It's over, Marcus. Drop your weapons and surrender."

Marcus glanced at his team, then back at Walker. Slowly, he raised his hands, a defeated smile playing on his lips. "You win this round, Detective. But don't think for a second that this is the end."

As the NYPD team moved in to arrest Marcus and his crew, Walker felt a sense of relief wash over him. The heist had been thwarted, and the Diamond District was safe for now. But he knew Marcus Kane was not a man who gave up easily.

As Marcus was led away in handcuffs, he locked eyes with Walker. "I'll be back, Detective. And next time, you won't see me coming."

Walker nodded, unphased. "We'll be ready."

The Diamond District returned to its usual hustle and bustle the next day, but the memory of the near-heist lingered. Walker and Sarah continued their patrols, ever vigilant, knowing that as long as there were diamonds on 47th Street, there would always be those looking to steal them.

CHAPTER 04

THE AFTERMATH

The following morning, the Diamond District was buzzing with gossip and speculation about the thwarted heist. Jewelers, traders, and shoppers exchanged excited whispers, recounting the dramatic events of the previous night. Word spread quickly: the infamous Marcus Kane had been captured, thanks to the quick action of the NYPD.

Detective James Walker and Detective Sarah Martinez walked the streets, their presence reassuring to the merchants and shoppers who had witnessed the district's near brush with disaster. The atmosphere was a mix of relief and heightened vigilance, as everyone knew that where there was one Marcus Kane, there were others waiting in the wings.

At the precinct, the arrest of Marcus and his crew was the talk of the day. Walker and Sarah sat in the briefing room, going over the details of the operation with their captain.

"Excellent work, both of you," Captain Daniels said, his gruff voice tinged with satisfaction. "But we can't rest easy yet. Marcus Kane is a resourceful criminal, and he's got connections. We need to be prepared for any retaliatory moves."

Walker nodded. "We're already stepping up patrols and coordinating with local security firms. The merchants are on high alert, and we're making sure they have the support they need."

Sarah added, "And we've got Rachel keeping an ear to the ground. She's proven to be a valuable asset. Any whispers about another heist, and we'll be on it."

Captain Daniels leaned back in his chair, rubbing his chin thoughtfully. "Good. Keep me posted on any developments. And Walker, Martinez — stay sharp. This isn't over."

Meanwhile, in a high-security holding cell, Marcus Kane sat on the edge of his cot, his mind racing. The capture had been a setback, but it wasn't the end. He had been in tight spots before and had always found a way out. This time would be no different.

As he stared at the gray walls of his cell, Marcus began to formulate a plan. He knew he had to act quickly, leveraging his connections and resources to regain his freedom. The first step was to communicate with his lawyer, who was more than just a legal advisor but a crucial part of his criminal network.

Back in the Diamond District, Rachel was trying to return to some semblance of normalcy. Her shop had reopened, and she busied herself with customers and inventory, but the events of the past few days weighed heavily on her mind. She had played a critical role in stopping Marcus, but she knew it wasn't over.

Rachel was in the middle of arranging a display when her phone buzzed. It was a text from Walker: "Need to see you. Urgent. Can you come to the precinct?"

Her heart skipped a beat. She quickly finished up with her customer and locked up her shop, making her way to the precinct with a sense of foreboding.

When she arrived, Walker and Sarah were waiting for her in the briefing room. Their expressions were serious, but there was also a hint of urgency.

"Rachel, thanks for coming," Walker said, motioning for her to sit. "We have some new information, and we need your help again."

Rachel nodded, her anxiety rising. "What's going on?"

Sarah handed her a file. "We've intercepted some communications that suggest Marcus's crew is planning something. They're trying to regroup and possibly break him out."

Rachel's eyes widened. "Break him out? But how?"

Walker leaned forward. "That's what we're trying to figure out. We need you to keep your ear to the ground. If you hear anything – anything at all – let us know immediately."

Rachel took a deep breath, her resolve hardening. "I will. I promise."

As the days passed, the NYPD intensified its surveillance and undercover operations in the Diamond District. Walker and Sarah were constantly on the move, coordinating with their informants and monitoring any suspicious activity.

One evening, while reviewing surveillance footage, Sarah spotted something unusual. "Walker, take a look at this."

Walker joined her at the monitor, watching as a group of men loitered near one of the high-end jewelry stores. They seemed out of place, their movements furtive and their expressions tense.

"Those guys don't look like typical shoppers," Walker observed. "Let's get a team down there and see what they're up to."

Rachel was closing up her shop for the night when she noticed a familiar face in the crowd. It was one of Marcus's men, someone she had seen during their brief encounters. Her heart raced as she watched him converse with another man, their expressions were serious.

Quickly, she grabbed her phone and texted Walker: "Just saw one of Marcus's men near my shop. Looks like they're planning something."

Walker responded almost immediately: "Get to a safe place. We're on our way."

Rachel slipped out the back door and hurried to a nearby café, keeping an eye on the street. Moments later, she saw Walker and Sarah arrive with a team of officers. They moved swiftly, surrounding the men and apprehending them without incident.

Back at the precinct, Walker and Sarah interrogated the suspects. One of them, a young man named Tony, seemed particularly nervous.

"Listen, Tony," Walker said, leaning in. "You're in deep trouble. But if you cooperate, we can help you. Tell us what Marcus is planning."

Tony hesitated, his eyes darting around the room. Finally, he sighed. "All right. They're planning to hit a transport convoy that's moving some high-value diamonds out of the district. They think it'll be easier to intercept the convoy than breaking into another vault."

Sarah exchanged a glance with Walker. "When is this going down?"

"Tomorrow night," Tony replied. "They've got the route mapped out and everything."

Walker stood up, his expression grim. "All right. We'll take it from here."

The next night, the NYPD was ready. They had set up a decoy convoy and strategically positioned their units along the planned route. Walker and Sarah were in an unmarked car, their eyes scanning the dark streets.

As the convoy moved out, a tense silence fell over the team. Minutes passed, each one stretching into what felt like an eternity. Then, they saw movement.

A black van sped towards the convoy, cutting in front of the lead vehicle. Armed men jumped out, ready to seize the diamonds. But instead of defenseless couriers, they found themselves facing a well-armed SWAT team.

"Freeze! NYPD!" Walker shouted, stepping out of the car with his weapon drawn.

The would-be robbers hesitated, realizing they had walked into a trap. One by one, they dropped their weapons and surrendered.

Back at the precinct, Walker and Sarah debriefed with Captain Daniels. The operation had been a success, and the threat to the Diamond District had been neutralized, at least for now.

Rachel, who had been anxiously waiting for news, breathed a sigh of relief when she received Walker's text: "We got them. It's over."

She smiled, feeling a sense of closure and a newfound resolve. She had played a part in protecting her community, and she knew that she would always be vigilant, ready to help keep the Diamond District safe.

Walker and Sarah, though relieved, knew that their work was never truly done. The city was full of challenges and dangers, but together, they were ready to face whatever came next.

CHAPTER 05

THE QUIET BEFORE THE STORM

With Marcus Kane and his crew behind bars, the Diamond District began to settle back into its familiar rhythm. The merchants, while still cautious, started to relax. The heightened police presence reassured them, and business picked up once again.

Detective James Walker and Detective Sarah Martinez were still vigilant. They knew Marcus Kane's arrest was a significant victory, but their instincts told them it was only a matter of time before another threat emerged.

Walker sat in his office, poring over case files and updating reports. Sarah entered a fresh cup of coffee in her hand.

"Morning, James," she said, setting the coffee down. "You look like you didn't sleep much."

Walker rubbed his eyes and took a sip of the coffee. "Thanks, Sarah. Just trying to stay on top of everything. I've got a bad feeling that we haven't seen the last of Marcus Kane."

Sarah nodded, taking a seat across from him. "Yeah, I feel it too. But for now, we've got to keep our focus on maintaining the peace we've restored."

Just then, Rachel walked in, her face a mixture of relief and lingering concern. "Good morning, Detectives. I wanted to thank you for everything you've done. The district feels safer already."

Walker smiled. "We're just doing our job, Rachel. And you've been a tremendous help. Without your information, we might not have been able to stop Marcus."

Rachel smiled, though her eyes betrayed her worry. "I just hope things stay quiet for a while. I'm not sure how much more excitement the district can handle."

Over the next few weeks, the Diamond District enjoyed a period of relative calm. Walker and Sarah continued their patrols, maintaining a visible presence and checking in regularly with the merchants. They also followed up on leads and monitored the activities of any known associates of Marcus Kane.

One afternoon, while reviewing surveillance footage, Sarah noticed something unusual. "Walker, come take a look at this."

Walker joined her at the monitor, watching as a group of unfamiliar men entered a jewelry store. They were well-dressed and appeared to be potential customers, but their behavior seemed off.

"Do we know who they are?" Walker asked.

Sarah shook her head. "Not yet. But they don't look like our usual clientele. I've flagged their faces for recognition. Let's see if we get any hits."

Later that evening, Walker and Sarah met with Captain Daniels to discuss their findings.

"These men showed up on our radar," Walker explained, showing the captain the footage. "They're not regulars in the district, and something about them feels wrong."

Captain Daniels studied the footage, his expression thoughtful. "Keep an eye on them. If they're up to something, we need to be ready."

The following day, Rachel received an unexpected visitor at her shop. It was one of the men from the surveillance footage, a tall, well-dressed man with piercing blue eyes.

"Good morning," he said with a charming smile. "I'm interested in some of your more exclusive pieces. I've heard you have an excellent selection."

Rachel forced a polite smile, her instincts on high alert. "Of course. Please, take a look."

As the man browsed, Rachel discreetly activated the silent alarm under her counter, alerting Walker and Sarah. Within minutes, they were on their way.

The man lingered, asking detailed questions about the security measures and inventory. Rachel answered as best she could, her heart racing. She knew she needed to keep him talking until Walker and Sarah arrived.

"These are exquisite pieces," the man said, holding up a diamond necklace. "Your security must be top-notch to protect such valuable items."

Rachel nodded. "Yes, we take security very seriously here."

Just then, Walker and Sarah entered the shop, their expressions calm but watchful. Walker approached the man, his badge visible. "Good afternoon. Is there something we can help you with?"

The man's smile faltered for a moment before he regained his composure. "Just browsing. I was interested in the security measures as well. It's always fascinating to see how these valuable items are protected."

Sarah stepped forward, her tone friendly but firm. "I'm Detective Sarah Martinez, and this is Detective James Walker. We'd like to ask you a few questions if you don't mind."

The man's eyes flickered with a hint of irritation, but he nodded. "Of course, Detective. I'm happy to cooperate."

Back at the precinct, the man introduced himself as Alexander Grey, a security consultant. His credentials checked out, but something about his demeanor left Walker and Sarah unconvinced.

"We appreciate your cooperation, Mr. Grey," Walker said, studying him closely. "But we'd like to know more about why you're interested in our district."

Alexander's smile didn't reach his eyes. "As I said, I'm a security consultant. I'm always looking for new challenges and opportunities. The Diamond District is renowned for its high-value assets, and I'm considering expanding my services here."

Sarah nodded, though she remained skeptical. "We'll be in touch if we have any more questions. Thank you for your time."

As Alexander left, Walker turned to Sarah. "Something's off about him. We need to keep an eye on him."

Sarah agreed. "I'll run a deeper background check and see what we can dig up."

Days turned into weeks, and the presence of Alexander Grey lingered like a shadow over the Diamond District. Walker and Sarah kept tabs on him, watching his movements and investigating his connections.

One evening, as Walker reviewed the latest reports, his phone rang. It was Rachel, her voice tense.

"James, I've been hearing some whispers. People are saying that Alexander is planning something big. I don't have all the details, but I thought you should know."

Walker thanked her and hung up, his mind racing. He called Sarah and briefed her on the situation.

"We need to act fast," Walker said. "If Alexander is planning something, we can't afford to be caught off guard."

Sarah nodded. "Let's get the team together and start putting the pieces together. We've got to stop this before it starts."

As they prepared for the next phase of their investigation, Walker and Sarah knew that the quiet they had enjoyed was about to be shattered. The storm was coming, and they needed to be ready for whatever Alexander Grey had in store.

CHAPTER 06

THE INVESTIGATION

Detective James Walker and Detective Sarah Martinez wasted no time assembling their team. The precinct buzzed with a renewed sense of urgency as officers reviewed the latest intelligence and strategized their next steps.

Walker stood at the front of the briefing room, addressing his team. "We have credible information that Alexander Grey is planning something big. Our priority is to figure out what he's up to and stop him before he can act. Keep your eyes and ears open, and report any suspicious activity immediately."

Sarah distributed surveillance photos and background checks. "We've got known associates of Grey identified. Some have criminal records, others are clean. We need to monitor all of them."

The team dispersed, and each officer was assigned specific tasks. Walker and Sarah headed out to the Diamond District, their first stop being Rachel's shop.

Rachel greeted them with a worried smile. "I'm glad you came. There's been a lot of talk, and people are on edge. I've noticed a few unfamiliar faces around the district lately."

Walker nodded. "We're here to check in and gather any information we can. Anything you've heard, no matter how small, could be useful."

Rachel led them to the back of her shop, where she had been keeping notes on the various comings and goings she had observed. "I've seen these guys around," she said, pointing to the surveillance photos. "They've been asking a lot of questions about security, inventory, and shipment schedules."

Sarah took detailed notes. "We'll follow up on these leads. Rachel, if you see or hear anything else, contact us immediately."

Rachel nodded. "Of course. I just want to make sure the district stays safe."

As Walker and Sarah continued their patrol, they stopped by other shops and spoke with merchants. The feedback was consistent: people were uneasy, and there were unfamiliar faces asking probing questions.

Back at the precinct, the team compiled all the information they had gathered. It was clear that something was in the works, but the specifics remained elusive.

Walker stared at the evidence board, deep in thought. "We need to find a way to draw Grey out. If we can catch him in the act, we'll have a better chance of shutting him down for good."

Sarah agreed. "What if we set up a decoy? Something valuable enough to tempt him into making a move?"

Walker's eyes lit up. "That's a good idea. We can work with a few of the jewelers to set up a fake shipment. Make it look real enough to lure him in."

They presented the plan to Captain Daniels, who gave his approval. "Make sure you have all the contingencies in place. We can't afford any slip-ups."

Over the next few days, Walker and Sarah meticulously planned the decoy operation. They coordinated with the jewelers to create a believable scenario and enlisted additional officers to ensure everything went smoothly.

The night of the operation, the tension was palpable. Walker and Sarah were stationed in an unmarked van, monitoring the fake shipment as it made its way through the district.

"All units, be advised," Walker said over the radio. "Stay alert and be ready to move at a moment's notice."

As the convoy neared a predetermined intersection, a black SUV cut in front of it, blocking its path. Walker's heart raced as he watched several men jump out, weapons drawn.

"Move in!" he shouted, leaping from the van with his weapon ready.

Officers swarmed the area, surrounding the would-be robbers. The men hesitated, realizing they were outnumbered and outgunned.

"Drop your weapons!" Sarah commanded, her voice steady.

One by one, the men complied, lowering their guns and raising their hands. Walker approached the SUV and opened the door, pulling Alexander Grey out.

"Game over, Grey," Walker said, cuffing him. "You're under arrest."

Grey's eyes blazed with fury, but he said nothing as he was led away.

Back at the precinct, Walker and Sarah processed the arrests. The operation had been a success, and the threat to the Diamond District had been neutralized once again.

Captain Daniels met them in the briefing room, a rare smile on his face. "Excellent work, both of you. You handled this perfectly."

Walker nodded. "Thanks, Captain. But we couldn't have done it without the team — and without Rachel's help."

Sarah added, "We need to stay vigilant. There's always another threat around the corner."

As they wrapped up their reports, Walker felt a sense of satisfaction. They had protected their city and kept the Diamond District safe. But he knew this was just one victory in an ongoing battle. Together with Sarah and their team, he was ready to face whatever challenges lay ahead.

CHAPTER 07

THE UNEXPECTED TWIST

With Alexander Grey behind bars and his crew dismantled the Diamond District began to breathe a collective sigh of relief. The merchants, once again, could focus on their businesses, and the streets regained their vibrant, bustling energy. However, Detectives James Walker and Sarah Martinez knew better than to let their guard down.

Walker sat in his office, staring at the case files. Despite their recent success, something gnawed at him. He felt that they were missing a crucial piece of the puzzle. His thoughts were interrupted by a knock on the door. It was Sarah.

"Got a minute?" she asked, stepping in.

"Of course. What's up?"

Sarah closed the door behind her and took a seat. "I've been going over the details of Grey's operation, and something doesn't add up. For someone as meticulous as him, his plan seemed... too straightforward."

Walker leaned back in his chair, considering her words. "You think there's more to it?"

Sarah nodded. "I do. I think Grey might have been a decoy – a distraction for something bigger."

Just then, Walker's phone buzzed. It was Rachel. Her voice was tense and hurried. "James, I just overheard something. I think there's another heist planned – something much bigger. They mentioned 'The Manhattan Star.'"

Walker's eyes widened. The Manhattan Star was one of the largest and most valuable diamonds in the world, housed in a highly secure vault at a prestigious jeweler's in the Diamond District.

"Thanks, Rachel. Stay safe. We'll take it from here." He hung up and turned to Sarah. "We need to move fast. If Grey was a distraction, the real target is The Manhattan Star."

The precinct buzzed with activity as Walker and Sarah briefed the team. They outlined the potential threat and the importance of securing The Manhattan Star. Captain Daniels authorized a full-scale operation, coordinating with private security firms and the jeweler's security team.

"We're dealing with professionals," Walker said, addressing the officers. "They'll be prepared for anything. We need to be one step ahead."

Sarah added, "We'll set up a perimeter around the jewelers and monitor all entry points. We'll have undercover officers inside, ready to respond at a moment's notice."

As night fell, the Diamond District seemed to hold its breath. Walker, Sarah, and their team were in position, their eyes scanning the streets and alleys for any sign of trouble. The jeweler's shop, where The Manhattan Star was housed, was a fortress of security measures, but they knew the stakes were high.

Walker and Sarah were stationed in an unmarked van, their eyes glued to the surveillance monitors. The minutes ticked by, each one feeling like an hour. Then, just after midnight, Sarah spotted something on the screen.

"Walker, look at this," she said, pointing to a group of men approaching the jeweler's back entrance. They moved with precision, their faces obscured by masks.

"They're here," Walker muttered, grabbing his radio. "All units, be advised. We have visual confirmation of suspects approaching the target. Move in."

The team sprang into action, surrounding the building and cutting off all escape routes. The suspects, realizing they had been caught, tried to force their way inside, triggering alarms and security measures. A firefight ensued, bullets ricocheting off the building's reinforced walls.

Walker and Sarah, leading the charge, moved swiftly through the chaos. They managed to corner one of the suspects, a tall man with a cold, calculating gaze.

"Hands up!" Walker shouted, his gun trained on the man.

The suspect hesitated, then smirked. "You think this is over, Detective? This is just the beginning."

With a sudden, fluid motion, he reached into his jacket, pulling out a device. Before Walker could react, the man pressed a button, and a deafening explosion rocked the street. Smoke and debris filled the air, and the man used the chaos to disappear into the night.

Back at the precinct, Walker and Sarah debriefed with Captain Daniels. The suspects had been part of a larger network, more organized and dangerous than they had anticipated. The explosion had been a diversion, allowing the mastermind to escape.

"We're dealing with a new player," Walker said grimly. "Someone who's willing to go to extreme lengths to get what they want."

Sarah nodded. "And they've got resources. We need to identify them and dismantle their operation before they strike again."

Captain Daniels looked at them, his expression serious. "You've got your work cut out for you. Keep digging, and follow every lead. We can't let this escalate."

As Walker and Sarah left the precinct, the weight of their new mission hung heavy in the air. The Diamond District might have been spared, but the battle was far from over. They knew that the quiet before the storm had passed, and now they were in the eye of the hurricane.

"We'll get them," Walker said, determination in his voice. "Whoever they are, we'll bring them down."

Sarah nodded, her resolve just as strong. "Together, we'll find the mastermind and end this once and for all."

As they walked into the night, the city's lights flickering around them, they knew that the hunt had only just begun.

CHAPTER 08

A NEW LEAD

The events of the previous night left the Diamond District on edge once again. The explosion had not only rattled the buildings but also the nerves of the merchants and residents. The streets, usually bustling with energy, were subdued, filled with cautious whispers and nervous glances.

Detective James Walker and Detective Sarah Martinez were back in their office early the next morning, sorting through the mountain of evidence collected from the scene of the explosion. The pieces of the puzzle were starting to come together, but there were still many gaps to fill.

"We need to find out who these guys are working for," Walker said, frustration evident in his voice. "And fast. They're clearly well-funded and organized."

Sarah nodded, her eyes scanning through the photos and documents spread out on the desk. "I've been looking into the device used in the explosion. It's sophisticated—military grade. Whoever is behind this has serious resources."

Just then, their colleague, Detective Mike Reynolds, entered the room. "Hey, I think I might have something," he said, holding up a piece of paper. "I ran a check on the suspect you cornered last night. His name is Viktor Sokolov, a known associate of the Russian mafia."

Walker took the paper and read through the information. "This complicates things. If the Russian mafia is involved, we're dealing with an international syndicate."

Sarah sighed. "Which means we're not just looking at local players. This is much bigger."

The team called an emergency meeting to discuss their findings and plan their next steps. Captain Daniels was there, his expression grim but determined.

"We need to coordinate with federal agencies," he said. "If the Russian mafia is involved, we'll need all the resources we can get."

Walker nodded. "Agreed. We also need to tighten security around the Diamond District. If they're planning something bigger, we have to be ready."

Over the next few days, Walker and Sarah worked tirelessly, liaising with federal agents and digging deeper into Viktor Sokolov's background. They discovered that Sokolov had been seen with a mysterious figure known only as "The Broker," a notorious middleman for high-stakes criminals.

"The Broker," Walker mused, reading through the file. "He's the key. If we can find him, we can get to the mastermind."

Sarah agreed. "But finding him won't be easy. He's a ghost. No digital footprint, no known aliases. Just a shadow in the criminal underworld."

That evening, Walker received a call from an old informant, a former hacker named Ian who had turned his life around and now ran a small cybersecurity firm. "James, I heard you're looking for The Broker," Ian said, his voice low and cautious.

"Yeah, we are," Walker replied. "Do you have any information?"

"I might," Ian said. "Meet me at our usual spot in an hour. And come alone."

Walker informed Sarah and Captain Daniels before heading out. The usual spot was a quiet café on the outskirts of the city, where Walker and Ian had met many times over the years.

Ian was already there when Walker arrived, sitting in a corner booth with a laptop open in front of him. He looked up as Walker approached and gestured for him to sit.

"I've been digging into the dark web," Ian began. "There's been a lot of chatter about a major deal going down. Word is, The Broker is brokering a deal for a massive diamond heist. The buyer is willing to pay a fortune for The Manhattan Star."

Walker leaned forward, his heart racing. "Do you know where this deal is happening?"

Ian nodded, pulling up a map on his laptop. "It's going down in two days at an abandoned warehouse in the industrial district. But be careful, James. These guys are dangerous."

"Thanks, Ian," Walker said, standing up. "You've been a great help."

Back at the precinct, Walker relayed the information to Sarah and Captain Daniels. "We need to plan a raid," he said. "This is our chance to catch The Broker and shut this operation down."

Sarah was already making notes. "We'll need SWAT and backup from the feds. We can't go in unprepared."

Captain Daniels agreed. "I'll make the calls. Let's make sure this is airtight. We only get one shot at this."

On the day of the raid, the team gathered for a final briefing. The tension was palpable as Walker and Sarah reviewed the plan. They would approach the warehouse from multiple angles, ensuring there were no escape routes for the suspects.

"Remember," Walker said, his voice steady. "Our priority is to capture The Broker and gather as much evidence as we can. Stay sharp and stay safe."

As they moved into position, the sun began to set, casting long shadows across the industrial district. Walker and Sarah led their team, silently approaching the warehouse.

Inside, they could hear the murmur of voices and the clinking of glasses. Walker signaled for the team to move in, and they burst through the doors, weapons drawn.

"Freeze! NYPD!" Walker shouted, scanning the room.

The suspects were caught off guard, some dropping their weapons, others trying to flee. The team moved swiftly, securing the area and apprehending the criminals.

In the midst of the chaos, Walker spotted a man slipping through a side door. He signaled to Sarah, and they pursued him, catching up to him in a dimly lit corridor.

"Stop right there!" Sarah shouted, raising her gun.

The man turned, his face obscured by shadows. "You're too late, Detectives," he said with a chilling calmness. "This isn't over."

Walker stepped closer, recognizing the face from the file. "The Broker, I presume."

The man smirked but said nothing. Walker and Sarah cuffed him and led him back to the main area, where the rest of the team was securing the scene.

Back at the precinct, The Broker was booked and taken into custody. Walker and Sarah knew that this arrest was just the beginning. They had a long road ahead to unravel the entire network and bring all the players to justice.

As they sat in the briefing room, exhausted but relieved, Captain Daniels entered with a rare smile. "Excellent work, both of you. We've made a significant dent in their operation today."

Walker nodded, his mind already racing with the next steps. "We've got a lot of work to do, but we're on the right track."

Sarah agreed. "We'll keep digging until we've taken down every last one of them."

As they left the precinct that night, the city lights twinkling around them, Walker and Sarah felt a renewed sense of purpose. They knew the battle was far from over, but they were ready to face whatever challenges lay ahead, determined to protect the Diamond District and bring justice to those who sought to disrupt its peace.

CHAPTER 09

DEEPER INTO THE WEB

The arrest of The Broker marked a significant milestone in the investigation, but Detectives James Walker and Sarah Martinez knew the battle was far from over. The Broker's capture was merely the tip of the iceberg, and they had a vast criminal network to dismantle.

The next morning, Walker and Sarah were back at the precinct, reviewing the evidence collected from the raid. Their immediate goal was to extract as much information as possible from The Broker.

"We need to get him to talk," Walker said, looking over the interrogation files. "If we can find out who he's working for, we can start taking down the rest of the organization."

Sarah nodded. "I'll arrange the interrogation room. Let's see if we can break him."

The Broker, a man in his late forties with a calm demeanor and piercing eyes, was led into the interrogation room. Walker and Sarah sat across from him, their expressions serious but controlled.

"Let's cut to the chase," Walker began. "We know you're connected to a major criminal syndicate. Tell us who you're working for, and things might go easier for you."

The Broker leaned back, a smirk playing on his lips. "I have nothing to say."

Sarah leaned forward, her voice cold. "You're looking at serious time, Broker. Cooperate, and we can talk about a deal."

He shrugged. "You think I'm afraid of prison? I've been in worse places."

Walker exchanged a glance with Sarah. They needed a different approach. "You've got people depending on you, don't you? Family, maybe? Think about what happens to them if you go away for life."

For a moment, The Broker's smirk faltered, but he quickly regained his composure. "Nice try, Detective. But you don't scare me."

Hours passed, and The Broker remained tight-lipped. Frustrated but not defeated, Walker and Sarah regrouped to devise a new strategy. They decided to dig deeper into The Broker's background, hoping to find leverage.

Walker contacted Ian, their informant. "We need more information on The Broker. Anything we can use to get him to talk."

Ian got to work, sifting through layers of encrypted data and hidden networks. After several hours, he called Walker with a breakthrough. "I found something. The Broker has a daughter, Emily. She's been living under a different name, but I traced her. She's a student at Columbia University."

Walker felt a glimmer of hope. "Thanks, Ian. This might be exactly what we need."

Armed with this new information, Walker and Sarah returned to the interrogation room. Walker placed a photo of Emily on the table in front of The Broker.

"Recognize her?" Walker asked, his tone gentle but firm.

The Broker's eyes widened for a split second before he masked his reaction. "What do you want?"

"Your cooperation," Sarah said. "Help us, and we can make sure she's safe."

The Broker looked at the photo, then back at the detectives. For the first time, he seemed genuinely conflicted. "What do you want to know?"

Walker leaned in. "Who's running this operation? Who's the mastermind?"

The Broker sighed, his resistance crumbling. "All right. But you have to promise me she'll be safe."

"You have our word," Sarah assured him.

The Broker took a deep breath. "The mastermind is a man named Viktor Ivanov. He's a high-ranking member of the Russian mafia, based out of Moscow. He's been orchestrating these heists from behind the scenes, using people like me to do his dirty work."

Walker's mind raced. "Do you have any contact information? Locations?"

"He uses secure lines, but I have a burner phone with his number. It's in my apartment."

Walker and Sarah shared a look of triumph. "Thank you. We'll take it from here."

Back at the precinct, the team analyzed the new information. Captain Daniels was briefed on the situation and authorized an international collaboration with law enforcement agencies to track down Viktor Ivanov.

"We're making progress," Daniels said. "But we need to tread carefully. Ivanov is dangerous and well-connected."

Walker nodded. "We'll coordinate with the feds and Interpol. We can't let him slip through our fingers."

As the days passed, the investigation gained momentum. Federal agents raided The Broker's apartment, retrieving the burner phone and other crucial evidence. Walker and Sarah worked tirelessly, piecing together Ivanov's network and mapping out his operations.

Their efforts led to a breakthrough when they intercepted a communication between Ivanov and one of his associates, detailing a planned heist in Europe. The team knew they had to act quickly to prevent another disaster.

Walker and Sarah found themselves on a plane to Moscow, coordinating with Russian authorities to apprehend Ivanov. The tension was palpable as they prepared for the operation.

"We've got one shot at this," Walker said. "Let's make it count."

The raid on Ivanov's hideout was swift and decisive. Russian special forces, along with Walker and Sarah, stormed the compound, catching Ivanov and his men off guard. After a brief but intense standoff, Ivanov was captured, his empire crumbling around him.

Back in New York, the news of Ivanov's capture was met with relief and celebration. The Diamond District could finally breathe easy, knowing the mastermind behind the heists was behind bars.

Walker and Sarah returned home, exhausted but triumphant. They knew the fight against crime was never truly over, but they had won a significant victory.

As they sat in their favorite diner, enjoying a much-needed break, Walker raised his coffee cup. "To justice."

Sarah clinked her cup against his. "To justice."

The city's lights twinkled outside a testament to the resilience and determination of those who fought to protect it. Walker and Sarah knew there would always be challenges ahead, but they were ready to face them, together.

CHAPTER 10

REPERCUSSIONS

The arrest of Viktor Ivanov sent shockwaves through the criminal underworld. The Russian mafia, known for its ruthlessness and influence, was reeling from the loss of one of its top operatives. Back in New York, Detectives James Walker and Sarah Martinez were hailed as heroes, their efforts bringing a renewed sense of security to the Diamond District.

However, the aftermath of the operation revealed deeper complexities. Walker and Sarah were aware that removing Ivanov was only the beginning. The void left by his capture could lead to a power struggle within the mafia, and they needed to remain vigilant.

In the days following their return, Walker and Sarah were inundated with debriefings, media interviews, and commendations. While the recognition was gratifying, both detectives remained focused on their ongoing mission.

Captain Daniels called them into his office for a strategy meeting. "We've dealt a significant blow to the Russian mafia, but we need to anticipate their next move. Ivanov's underlings won't sit idly by."

Walker nodded. "Agreed. We should increase our surveillance and intelligence efforts. We need to be ahead of any retaliatory actions."

Sarah added, "We should also protect anyone who could be a target for retribution, especially those who helped us."

Daniels concurred. "Let's put a plan in place. We've made significant progress, but we can't let our guard down."

One evening, as Walker was reviewing case files at his apartment, his phone buzzed. It was Ian, their informant. His voice was urgent and tense.

"James, we've got a problem. I've been monitoring the dark web and there's a lot of chatter about retribution. Ivanov's associates are planning to hit back, and they're targeting people close to you."

Walker's heart sank. "Do you have any specifics?"

"I've traced some communications that suggest they're targeting your family, James. They know about your sister and her kids."

Fear gripped Walker. "Thanks, Ian. I owe you. Stay safe."

Walker immediately called his sister, Emma. "Emma, listen to me carefully. You need to get out of the city with the kids. Now."

Emma, sensing the urgency in his voice, didn't question him. "Okay, James. We'll leave tonight. But what's going on?"

"I'll explain everything later. Just go somewhere safe and stay there. I'll be in touch."

Walker called Sarah next, explaining the situation. "We need to protect our families. This isn't just about us anymore."

Sarah, equally concerned, agreed. "I'll make arrangements for my parents. We'll need to coordinate protection details with the captain."

They spent the next few hours organizing security for their loved ones, ensuring they were moved to secure locations. The reality of their profession had never felt so personal and perilous.

At the precinct, Walker and Sarah worked with Captain Daniels to establish a protective detail for their families and close associates. They also ramped up their efforts to track any movements from Ivanov's remaining network.

Days turned into weeks, and the tension was palpable. The threat of retaliation loomed over them like a dark cloud. But Walker and Sarah were determined to stay one step ahead.

One night, as Walker and Sarah were working late, Ian called again. "I've got something. There's a hit squad that's just arrived in New York. They're professionals, ex-military types. They've been seen around the Diamond District."

Walker's jaw tightened. "Thanks, Ian. We'll take it from here."

He hung up and turned to Sarah. "We need to move fast. Let's gather the team and head to the Diamond District. We can't let these guys get a foothold."

The team, already on high alert, quickly mobilized. They set up surveillance around key locations in the Diamond District, blending in with the late-night activity.

Walker and Sarah were positioned in an unmarked car, watching for any suspicious movements. Hours passed, and just as dawn began to break, they spotted a group of men matching Ian's description.

"They're here," Walker whispered. "Let's move."

The team converged on the suspects, who were in the midst of setting up for an attack. A firefight erupted, bullets flying as the hit squad tried to fight their way out. But Walker and his team were prepared, their training and coordination proving superior.

In the end, the hit squad was apprehended, and their plans foiled. The threat of retribution had been neutralized, but Walker and Sarah knew the fight against organized crime was far from over.

Back at the precinct, Captain Daniels commended their efforts. "You both handled this exceptionally well. We've sent a clear message that we won't back down."

Walker nodded, exhaustion and relief washing over him. "We've won this round, but we need to stay vigilant. They'll keep coming."

Sarah agreed. "We'll be ready. Whatever it takes."

As they left the precinct that night, the weight of their responsibilities hung heavy on their shoulders. But they knew they were making a difference, one battle at a time. And as long as they had each other, they were ready to face whatever challenges lay ahead.

The city's lights shimmered in the distance, a beacon of hope and resilience. Walker and Sarah walked side by side, united in their resolve to protect the city they loved and the people within it. The fight against crime was never-ending, but they were ready for the next chapter, whatever it might bring.

CHAPTER 11

UNSEEN CONNECTIONS

The Diamond District gradually returned to its vibrant self after the threat of retaliation had been neutralized. Detective James Walker and Detective Sarah Martinez remained vigilant, but the successful takedown of the hit squad provided a temporary reprieve.

Walker sat at his desk, sipping his coffee while reviewing reports. The precinct buzzed with activity, but his mind drifted to his family. He had managed to get them to safety, but the recent events underscored the constant danger they all faced.

Sarah walked in, a file in hand. "Got something interesting," she said, placing the file on Walker's desk. "I did some digging on Ivanov's network. There are some financial transactions that don't quite add up."

Walker flipped through the pages. "Money laundering?"

"Possibly," Sarah replied. "But it's more than that. It looks like they're using legitimate businesses as fronts. Jewelry stores, import-export firms, even a few tech companies."

Walker frowned. "If we can link these businesses to Ivanov, we can dismantle his entire operation. Let's focus on these leads."

Over the next few days, Walker and Sarah worked tirelessly, tracking financial records and piecing together the puzzle. They identified several businesses in the Diamond District and beyond that seemed to be connected to Ivanov's network.

One name stood out: Nikolai Petrov, a prominent businessman with ties to multiple industries. Petrov's clean public image contrasted sharply with the shady transactions they had uncovered.

"We need to dig deeper into Petrov," Walker said. "If he's involved, he could be the key to taking down the rest of Ivanov's network."

Their investigation led them to Petrov's main office, a sleek, modern building in Midtown Manhattan. Posing as potential clients, Walker and Sarah managed to secure a meeting with Petrov himself.

Petrov was a tall, imposing man with a charismatic presence. He welcomed them into his luxurious office, offering them drinks and engaging in small talk.

Walker started the conversation. "Mr. Petrov, we're interested in expanding our investments, and we've heard great things about your company."

Petrov smiled, his eyes sharp and calculating. "I'm always happy to discuss business opportunities. What areas are you interested in?"

Sarah leaned in. "We're particularly interested in your import-export business. We've heard it's very profitable."

Petrov's smile widened. "It is. We have some of the best connections and resources in the industry."

Walker exchanged a glance with Sarah before continuing. "We've also heard rumors about certain... side ventures. More lucrative, but less public."

Petrov's demeanor shifted slightly, a flicker of suspicion in his eyes. "I'm not sure what you're referring to."

Walker decided to push further. "We're willing to invest heavily, but we need assurances that our money will be secure. We've heard Ivanov's name mentioned in connection with your operations."

At the mention of Ivanov, Petrov's expression hardened. "I don't know what you're talking about. My businesses are legitimate."

Before the conversation could escalate, Walker and Sarah made their excuses and left, having gathered enough to warrant a deeper investigation into Petrov.

Back at the precinct, they presented their findings to Captain Daniels. "Petrov's involved, we're sure of it," Sarah said. "We need to gather more evidence to bring him down."

Daniels agreed. "We'll get warrants for surveillance and wiretaps. If Petrov is tied to Ivanov, we'll find the proof."

The next few weeks were a blur of covert operations and late-night stakeouts. Walker and Sarah monitored Petrov's businesses, documenting every suspicious transaction and interaction.

One night, while reviewing wiretap recordings, they hit the jackpot. Petrov was on the phone, discussing a shipment with one of Ivanov's known associates. The conversation was incriminating, revealing details of money laundering and smuggling operations.

"We've got him," Walker said, excitement and determination in his voice. "This is enough to take him down."

Armed with the new evidence, they obtained arrest warrants and prepared for a coordinated raid on Petrov's businesses. The operation involved multiple agencies, ensuring no stone was left unturned.

The raid was swift and efficient. Walker and Sarah led the charge, storming Petrov's office and securing crucial documents and computer files. Petrov was arrested, his calm demeanor replaced with outrage and fear.

"You can't do this!" Petrov shouted as he was led away in handcuffs. "You have no idea who you're dealing with!"

Walker looked him in the eye. "We know exactly who we're dealing with. Your empire is crumbling, and there's nothing you can do about it."

The arrest of Nikolai Petrov sent another shockwave through the criminal underworld. The evidence collected during the raid provided a treasure trove of information, leading to further arrests and the dismantling of Ivanov's network.

Back at the precinct, the atmosphere was one of triumph and relief. Walker and Sarah knew there were still battles to fight, but this victory was a significant step towards restoring peace and security.

Captain Daniels gathered the team for a brief celebration. "Excellent work, everyone. This is a major win for us and for the city."

Walker raised his glass. "To justice."

Sarah smiled. "And to the team that makes it happen."

As they clinked glasses, Walker and Sarah felt a renewed sense of purpose. The fight against crime was ongoing, but they were ready for whatever challenges lay ahead, knowing they had the skills and the resolve to protect their city.

CHAPTER 12

HIDDEN AGENDAS

With Nikolai Petrov behind bars and the dismantling of Ivanov's network well underway, Detectives James Walker and Sarah Martinez felt a cautious sense of victory. However, they knew the criminal underworld often had more layers than they initially perceived.

The precinct was buzzing with the aftermath of the recent successes. Officers were sorting through the vast amounts of data and evidence collected from Petrov's businesses, identifying further connections and leads. Walker and Sarah were in the thick of it, coordinating efforts and following up on new intelligence.

One morning, Sarah approached Walker with a grim expression. "James, we need to talk. I've been going through Petrov's financial records and found something disturbing."

Walker looked up from his desk, concern etched on his face. "What is it?"

Sarah handed him a folder. "There are significant transactions linked to a political figure. Councilman Richard Hayes. It looks like he's been receiving substantial sums from Petrov's companies."

Walker's eyes widened as he scanned the documents. "A councilman? This could blow the lid off a major corruption scandal."

"Exactly," Sarah replied. "We need to tread carefully. If Hayes is involved, he could have powerful allies."

Walker nodded, his mind racing. "Let's gather more evidence before we make any moves. We can't afford to tip him off prematurely."

They spent the next few days meticulously investigating Hayes' connections to Petrov. Their findings painted a troubling picture of corruption and collusion, suggesting that Hayes had been using his position to facilitate Petrov's operations in exchange for financial kickbacks.

Walker and Sarah decided to loop in Captain Daniels. "Captain, we've uncovered evidence that implicates

Councilman Hayes in Petrov's criminal activities," Walker explained. "This goes beyond organized crime. We're looking at political corruption."

Daniels rubbed his temples, the weight of the revelation evident. "This is serious. If we move on this, we'll be taking on some very powerful people."

"We know," Sarah said. "But we can't ignore this. We need to bring him down."

Daniels agreed. "All right. We'll need to work with Internal Affairs and the District Attorney's office. This has to be airtight."

The investigation into Councilman Hayes intensified, with Internal Affairs and the DA's office joining forces with Walker and Sarah. They gathered evidence through wiretaps, surveillance, and financial audits, ensuring every detail was meticulously documented.

One evening, while listening to a wiretap, Walker and Sarah caught a crucial conversation between Hayes and one of Petrov's associates. The conversation confirmed Hayes' involvement, discussing bribes and the manipulation of city contracts to benefit Petrov's businesses.

"This is it," Walker said, adrenaline coursing through him. "We have enough to bring him in."

The arrest of Councilman Richard Hayes made headlines, sending shockwaves through the city's political landscape. The evidence was overwhelming, and Hayes' once-sterling reputation was in tatters.

As Hayes was led away in handcuffs, he spat bitterly at Walker and Sarah. "You think you've won? This is far from over. There are others, more powerful than you can imagine."

Walker remained stoic. "We'll find them too. One by one."

The fallout from Hayes' arrest was immediate and far-reaching. Several other city officials were implicated in the scandal, leading to a series of resignations and arrests. The city was in an uproar, demanding accountability and transparency.

Walker and Sarah found themselves at the center of a media storm, their efforts lauded by the public but also scrutinized by those who feared further exposure.

Captain Daniels called them into his office. "You've done incredible work, both of you. But this investigation has rattled some very influential cages. We need to stay vigilant."

"We will," Sarah assured him. "We're not done yet."

Despite the ongoing turbulence, Walker and Sarah remained focused. The depth of the corruption they had uncovered hinted at an even larger network of collusion and criminal activity.

One evening, as they were poring over the latest documents, Ian called. "James, Sarah, I've been digging deeper into Petrov's network. There's another player you need to know about. A shadowy figure named Dmitri Volkov. He's even more dangerous than Ivanov and Petrov combined."

Walker's heart sank. "What do you have on him?"

"Not much yet, but I'm working on it. Be careful. This guy is connected at the highest levels, both in the criminal world and politically."

Walker and Sarah knew they were stepping into dangerous territory, but they were undeterred. The stakes were higher than ever, and the path ahead was fraught with peril. But they had come this far, and there was no turning back.

As they prepared for the next phase of their investigation, they reflected on how far they had come. The fight against corruption and crime was relentless, but they were driven by a deep sense of duty and justice.

The city's lights flickered in the night, a constant reminder of the challenges and dangers that lay ahead. But Walker and Sarah were ready to face them, together, as always.

Their resolve was unbreakable, their mission clear. They would uncover the truth, no matter the cost, and bring those who sought to corrupt and exploit the city to justice.

CHAPTER 13

THE SHADOW OF DMITRI VOLKOV

Detectives James Walker and Sarah Martinez knew that their investigation was entering its most dangerous phase yet. Dmitri Volkov was a name that struck fear into the hearts of many in the criminal underworld. His influence spanned continents, and his network was said to be nearly impenetrable.

The precinct was on high alert as they began digging into Volkov's activities. They had to tread carefully; Volkov was known for his ruthlessness and his ability to eliminate threats swiftly and without hesitation.

Walker and Sarah started by compiling all available intelligence on Volkov. They knew they needed more information to proceed. Walker contacted Ian, their trusted informant, who had been their lifeline in the criminal world.

"Ian, we need everything you can get on Dmitri Volkov. We're going after him," Walker said over a secure line.

Ian hesitated. "James, this guy is different. He's extremely dangerous. His network is vast and well-protected. But I'll do what I can. Just... be careful."

While Ian worked on gathering intel, Walker and Sarah began analyzing the information they already had. They found that Volkov's operations were not limited to New York; he had ties to several major cities across the globe. His network included drug trafficking, arms dealing, human trafficking, and high-stakes money laundering.

Their investigation also revealed that Volkov had several legitimate businesses that he used as fronts for his illegal activities. These included shipping companies, luxury car dealerships, and real estate firms. One name that kept appearing in their files was a high-end nightclub in Manhattan called "Eclipse."

Posing as potential investors, Walker and Sarah decided to pay a visit to Eclipse. The nightclub was known for its exclusivity and its clientele of wealthy elites and powerful figures.

Dressed to blend in with the crowd, they arrived at Eclipse on a busy Friday night. The bouncers gave them a cursory glance before allowing them entry. Inside, the club was a dazzling display of opulence, with chandeliers, velvet couches, and a state-of-the-art sound system.

They made their way to the bar, scanning the crowd for anyone who might be connected to Volkov. Sarah spotted a man in a tailored suit, sitting in a VIP section surrounded by bodyguards.

"That's Sergei Ivanov, Dmitri's right-hand man," she whispered to Walker. "If anyone can lead us to Volkov, it's him."

Walker and Sarah approached the VIP area, attempting to catch Sergei's attention. They managed to engage him in conversation, posing as wealthy investors looking to expand their business interests in New York.

Sergei was initially cautious, but their cover story was convincing. He agreed to a meeting the following day to discuss potential opportunities. As they left the club, Walker and Sarah knew they were getting closer to Volkov.

The next day, they met Sergei at an upscale restaurant in Midtown Manhattan. Over a lavish lunch, they discussed various business ventures. Walker and Sarah subtly steered the conversation towards Volkov, expressing admiration for his business acumen.

Sergei, clearly enjoying the flattery, began to open up. "Dmitri is a genius. He sees opportunities where others see obstacles. That's why he's so successful."

Walker nodded. "We've heard he's involved in some very lucrative ventures. We'd love to meet him and discuss how we can collaborate."

Sergei smiled. "Perhaps. Dmitri is very selective about his associates. But I can arrange a meeting, provided you prove your worth."

Walker and Sarah knew they had to tread carefully. They needed to gather enough evidence to bring Volkov down without tipping him off. They continued to play the role of eager investors, gaining Sergei's trust.

Meanwhile, Ian provided them with critical information about Volkov's operations. He had uncovered details about a major shipment of illegal arms scheduled to arrive in New York. This shipment was set to be a significant event in Volkov's network, and intercepting it could deal a significant blow to his operations.

With this new information, Walker and Sarah coordinated with Captain Daniels to set up a sting operation. They planned to intercept the shipment and use it as leverage to get closer to Volkov.

The night of the operation, the team was in position at the docks where the shipment was expected. Tensions were high as they waited for the signal. Finally, a convoy of trucks arrived, and the team moved in.

The raid was swift and decisive. They apprehended several of Volkov's men and secured the shipment. Among the evidence collected were documents that linked the operation directly to Volkov.

With the success of the sting operation, Walker and Sarah had the leverage they needed. They arranged another meeting with Sergei, this time presenting themselves as even more valuable allies.

Sergei, impressed by their apparent success, agreed to set up a meeting with Volkov. The meeting was to take place at a remote, secure location outside the city.

Walker and Sarah knew this would be their best chance to bring Volkov down. They prepared meticulously, coordinating with their team and ensuring they had all necessary precautions in place.

The day of the meeting, they traveled to the location, a secluded estate in the countryside. As they approached, they were met by armed guards who escorted them inside. The tension was palpable as they waited in an opulent sitting room.

Finally, Dmitri Volkov entered the room. He was a tall, imposing figure with an air of authority and menace. He studied Walker and Sarah with cold, calculating eyes.

"I understand you've been very eager to meet me," Volkov said, his voice smooth and dangerous.

Walker remained calm. "We're interested in opportunities that can be mutually beneficial. We've heard a lot about your operations and would like to discuss how we can be of service."

Volkov smiled, but there was no warmth in it. "I appreciate ambition. But trust is earned, not given. Prove to me that you're worth my time."

Walker and Sarah presented the intercepted shipment as a gesture of goodwill, explaining how they had managed to secure it and suggesting ways to expand Volkov's operations.

Volkov listened intently, his interest piqued. "You've done well. Perhaps there is potential here after all."

As the meeting progressed, Walker and Sarah gathered valuable intelligence about Volkov's network and operations. They knew they had to be careful, but they also saw an opportunity to dismantle his empire from within.

The meeting concluded with Volkov agreeing to a tentative partnership. Walker and Sarah left the estate, their minds racing with the possibilities and the dangers ahead.

Back in the city, they met with Captain Daniels to debrief and plan their next moves. The fight against Volkov was just beginning, but they were determined to see it through.

As they prepared for the challenges ahead, Walker and Sarah felt a renewed sense of purpose. They were up against one of the most dangerous criminals they had ever encountered, but they had come too far to back down now.

The city's lights flickered in the distance, a reminder of the battles they had fought and the ones still to come. Walker and Sarah were ready, their resolve unbreakable. They would bring Volkov down, no matter the cost.

THE DEEP DIVE

The meeting with Dmitri Volkov had gone better than expected, but Detectives James Walker and Sarah Martinez knew that gaining his trust was just the first step in a much larger, more perilous game. They needed to be meticulous, patient, and above all, ready for anything.

Back at the precinct, they pored over the information gathered from the meeting. Volkov had hinted at several operations and contacts that could prove invaluable in taking him down. They needed to map out these connections and prepare for their next move.

Walker and Sarah focused on Volkov's financial network, using the intercepted shipment as leverage. Ian, their trusted informant, had continued to dig deeper, providing them with crucial insights into Volkov's laundering schemes and offshore accounts.

"This is massive," Sarah said, highlighting a series of transactions. "These accounts are tied to some very influential figures. If we can trace this money, we might uncover more of Volkov's network."

Walker nodded. "We need to follow the money trail. It's risky, but if we can connect these dots, we'll have a solid case."

They started by targeting smaller players in Volkov's operation, flipping them to gain more information. This approach led them to Alexei Romanov, a mid-level operative who managed some of Volkov's financial transactions.

Walker and Sarah brought Romanov in for questioning. Initially defiant, Romanov's resolve weakened when presented with the overwhelming evidence against him.

"You can either help us and get a deal, or you go down with Volkov," Walker said, his tone firm. "Your choice."

Romanov hesitated, then finally agreed to cooperate. He revealed details about the laundering process, naming several shell companies and front businesses used by Volkov to move money undetected.

With Romanov's information, they secured warrants to raid these businesses. The operations were swift and precise, yielding a treasure trove of documents and electronic records. Each raid brought them closer to the heart of Volkov's empire.

One of the businesses, a seemingly legitimate shipping company, had files that detailed shipments of illicit goods disguised as legal cargo. This evidence linked Volkov to international smuggling and trafficking networks.

As they compiled the evidence, Walker and Sarah realized they were uncovering a web of corruption that extended far beyond New York. Volkov's influence reached into major cities worldwide, involving politicians, businessmen, and other criminals.

Captain Daniels called a meeting to assess their progress. "You've made incredible strides, but we need to be careful. Volkov has eyes and ears everywhere. We can't afford any mistakes."

Walker agreed. "We need to move quickly but cautiously. We have enough to disrupt his operations, but bringing him in will require airtight evidence."

Sarah added, "We're also dealing with high-level corruption. We need to ensure our own safety and that of our witnesses."

Daniels nodded. "Understood. We'll increase security and coordinate with federal agencies. This is bigger than us now."

As they prepared for the final phase of their operation, Walker and Sarah received a tip from Ian about an upcoming meeting between Volkov and several key players in his network. This meeting, set to take place in a private mansion outside the city, could provide the opportunity they needed to capture Volkov and his associates red-handed.

They devised a plan to infiltrate the meeting. Disguised as part of Volkov's security detail, Walker and Sarah would gain access to the mansion, gather evidence, and signal their team to move in at the right moment.

The night of the meeting, tension was palpable. Walker and Sarah arrived at the mansion, their nerves steeled for the task ahead. They passed through the rigorous security checks and entered the opulent estate.

Inside, the atmosphere was one of tense anticipation. High-ranking members of Volkov's network mingled, discussing their various illicit ventures. Volkov himself stood at the center, exuding an air of control and menace.

Walker and Sarah moved through the crowd, discreetly recording conversations and gathering intelligence. They noted the presence of several known criminals and corrupt officials, all deeply intertwined with Volkov's empire.

At the designated time, Walker signaled their team, who were positioned around the estate. The raid was swift and coordinated, taking Volkov and his associates by surprise. Armed agents stormed the mansion, securing key targets and seizing evidence.

Volkov, realizing the betrayal, turned to Walker and Sarah with a look of cold fury. "You think you've won? This is just the beginning. My reach is far greater than you can imagine."

Walker remained resolute. "Your reign of terror ends here, Volkov. It's over."

Volkov was taken into custody, along with several high-ranking members of his network. The evidence gathered during the raid was more than enough to bring charges against them, effectively dismantling a significant portion of his criminal empire.

Back at the precinct, the atmosphere was one of triumph mixed with caution. The arrest of Dmitri Volkov was a major victory, but they knew the fight against corruption and crime was far from over.

Captain Daniels addressed the team. "Outstanding work, everyone. This is a huge step forward, but we need to remain vigilant. There will always be more threats, more challenges. But together, we can overcome them."

Walker and Sarah exchanged a look of mutual respect and determination. They had faced incredible odds and emerged victorious, but their journey was ongoing.

As they left the precinct that night, the city's lights shone brightly, a symbol of the hope and resilience that guided their mission. They knew the path ahead would be difficult, but they were ready to face it, together, as always.

Their resolve was unbreakable, their commitment to justice unwavering. They had taken down one of the most dangerous criminals they had ever encountered, but they knew there were always more battles to fight, more truths to uncover.

And they were ready.

CHAPTER 15

THE AFTERMATH

The takedown of Dmitri Volkov was a significant victory for Detectives James Walker and Sarah Martinez, but it was not without consequences. The aftermath of the raid sent shockwaves through both the criminal underworld and the corridors of power. As the dust began to settle, the challenges of their victory became increasingly apparent.

The precinct was inundated with media inquiries and legal proceedings. The high-profile nature of Volkov's arrest meant that every move Walker and Sarah made was scrutinized by the public and the press. Captain Daniels had to manage not only the ongoing investigations but also the department's public image.

One morning, as they sifted through the endless paperwork and prepared for a series of depositions, Sarah looked at Walker, her expression weary but determined. "We've got Volkov, but his network is vast. We need to keep up the pressure."

Walker nodded, his thoughts mirroring hers. "Agreed. We can't let our guard down. There are still plenty of his associates out there, and they'll be looking to fill the power vacuum."

The first major court appearance for Volkov was a spectacle. The courtroom was packed with reporters, onlookers, and a heavy security presence. Volkov appeared defiant, his cold demeanor unwavering despite the overwhelming evidence against him.

Walker and Sarah sat in the front row, their presence a testament to their commitment to seeing justice served. The prosecution laid out a damning case, meticulously presenting the evidence they had gathered. It was clear that Volkov's reign was coming to an end, but the battle was far from over.

In the days following the court appearance, Walker and Sarah continued to work tirelessly. They focused on securing the testimonies of key witnesses and dismantling the remaining elements of Volkov's network. Each new arrest brought them closer to fully understanding the extent of his operations.

Ian, their informant, played a crucial role in this phase. His deep connections within the criminal underworld provided invaluable insights, leading to several successful raids and further arrests.

One evening, as they reviewed the latest intelligence, Ian contacted them with urgent news. "James, Sarah, you need to see this. I've uncovered plans for a retaliation strike. Volkov's loyalists are organizing something big. They're targeting the city's infrastructure to cause chaos and divert attention from their operations."

Realizing the gravity of the situation, Walker and Sarah sprang into action. They coordinated with Captain Daniels and other agencies to thwart the planned attacks. The city was placed on high alert, with increased security measures implemented across key locations.

The operation to prevent the attacks was intense. Walker and Sarah led a task force to intercept the loyalists before they could carry out their plans. It was a race against time, but their swift actions and strategic planning paid off.

The loyalists were apprehended in a series of coordinated raids, and their plans foiled. The city breathed a sigh of relief, but the incident served as a stark reminder of the ongoing threats they faced.

In the aftermath of the foiled attacks, the focus shifted to the broader implications of their victory. The takedown of Volkov and his network had not only disrupted organized crime but also exposed deep-seated corruption within the political and business sectors.

Walker and Sarah worked closely with federal investigators to root out these corrupt elements. Their efforts led to several high-profile arrests and resignations, sending a clear message that no one was above the law.

The media continued to cover the unfolding drama, painting Walker and Sarah as heroes in the fight against crime and corruption. While they appreciated the recognition, they remained focused on their mission.

As the months passed, the legal proceedings against Volkov and his associates moved forward. The evidence was overwhelming, and the prosecution's case was airtight. Volkov was found guilty on multiple counts, receiving a lengthy prison sentence that ensured he would no longer be a threat.

The city began to heal, the shadows of Volkov's reign gradually lifting. Walker and Sarah found a sense of closure, knowing they had made a significant impact. Their work had not only brought down a dangerous criminal but had also sparked a broader movement towards justice and transparency.

One evening, as they walked through the bustling streets of New York, Sarah turned to Walker. "We did it, James. We took down Volkov and made the city safer. But there's always more work to be done."

Walker smiled, his eyes reflecting the determination that had carried them through countless challenges. "You're right, Sarah. There's always more to do. But we've shown that we can make a difference. And we'll keep fighting, no matter what."

They stood for a moment, taking in the city they had sworn to protect. The lights of New York shone brightly, a testament to its resilience and the enduring spirit of its people.

Back at the precinct, Captain Daniels addressed the team. "We've achieved a great victory, but the fight against crime and corruption is ongoing. Let's continue to work together, stay vigilant, and uphold the values that define us."

Walker and Sarah looked around at their colleagues, feeling a deep sense of pride and camaraderie. They knew the path ahead would be challenging, but they were ready to face whatever came their way.

As they prepared for the next chapter in their careers, they felt a renewed sense of purpose. The battle against darkness was never-ending, but they were committed to shining a light, one step at a time.

Together, they would continue to protect and serve, driven by the unyielding belief that justice would prevail and that the city they loved would always endure.

CONCLUSION

The arrest and conviction of Dmitri Volkov marked the end of one of the most challenging cases in the careers of Detectives James Walker and Sarah Martinez. It was a hard-fought victory that reverberated throughout New York City, signaling a significant blow to organized crime and corruption. But as the city breathed a collective sigh of relief, Walker and Martinez knew that their work was far from over.

The takedown of Volkov had exposed a vast network of criminal activity that extended far beyond the confines of the Diamond District. It revealed the intricate connections between powerful figures, the deep-seated corruption in various sectors, and the relentless ambition that drove men like Marcus Kane. With each revelation, the detectives realized that they had merely scratched the surface of a much larger, more insidious problem.

Their victory, while substantial, was just the beginning of a new phase in their quest for justice. The city's underbelly still harbored countless secrets, and the power vacuum left by Volkov's fall threatened to unleash even more chaos. As Walker and Martinez stood on the precipice of this new challenge, they felt a renewed sense of purpose and resolve.

The journey ahead would be fraught with danger and uncertainty, but they were ready to face it together. Their commitment to protecting the city and upholding the law was unwavering, and they knew that the fight against crime and corruption was a never-ending battle. With their partnership stronger than ever, they prepared to dive deeper into the shadows, ready to shine a light on the darkest corners of New York City.

The story of the New York Diamond Heist on 47th Street had come to a close, but the legacy of their work would continue. Walker and Martinez were more than just detectives; they were guardians of justice, and their mission was far from complete. As they looked towards the future, they knew that the real work was only just beginning.

Introduction to Volume II: The Shadows Within

In the wake of Dmitri Volkov's arrest, New York City seemed to return to a semblance of normalcy. The Diamond District, once again bustling with business, glittered with the promise of prosperity and security. But beneath this façade of calm lay a brewing storm, a darkness that threatened to engulf the city in a new wave of crime and corruption.

Detectives James Walker and Sarah Martinez, hailed as heroes for their role in bringing down Volkov, knew that the peace was tenuous at best. The power vacuum left by Volkov's fall had created a volatile landscape, one that unscrupulous players were eager to exploit. As new alliances formed and old rivalries reignited, the detectives found themselves plunged into a world of intrigue and danger far greater than they had ever imagined.

Volume II: The Shadows Within delves deeper into the intricate web of crime that pervades New York City. It follows Walker and Martinez as they navigate a labyrinth of deceit, facing off against a new breed of adversaries who are as cunning as they are ruthless. The stakes are higher, the threats more insidious, and the line between friend and foe increasingly blurred.

As they pursue leads and uncover hidden truths, the detectives are forced to confront their own limitations and vulnerabilities. The challenges they face are not just external; they must also grapple with the personal costs of their dedication to justice. Relationships are tested, loyalties questioned, and their very identities as protectors of the law put to the ultimate test.

The Shadows Within is a story of resilience and determination, of the unyielding fight against the encroaching darkness. It explores the depths of human ambition and the enduring strength of those who choose to stand against it. In this new volume, Walker and Martinez must dig deeper than ever before, uncovering not just the criminal underworld but also the shadows within themselves.

Join them as they embark on this next chapter of their journey, where every decision carries weight, and every action has consequences. The battle for the soul of New York City continues, and the detectives must summon all their courage and ingenuity to prevail. The shadows are closing in, but as long as there is light, there is hope. And as long as there are people willing to fight for justice, the darkness will never win.

Welcome to Volume II: The Shadows Within. The journey into the heart of New York's most hidden secrets begins now.

www.ingramcontent.com/pod-product-compliance
Lightning Source LLC
Chambersburg PA
CBHW010424120726
47992CB00008B/3325